STORIES FROM GREEK TRAGEDIES

The *Oxford Progressive English Readers* series provides a wide range of reading for learners of English.

Each book in the series has been written to follow the strict guidelines of a syllabus, wordlist and structure list. The texts are graded according to these guidelines; Grade 1 at a 1,400 word level, Grade 2 at a 2,100 word level, Grade 3 at a 3,100 word level, Grade 4 at a 3,700 word level and Grade 5 at a 5,000 word level.

The latest methods of text analysis, using specially designed software, ensure that readability is carefully controlled at every level. Any new words which are vital to the mood and style of the story are explained within the text, and reoccur throughout for maximum reinforcement. New language items are also clarified by attractive illustrations.

Each book has a short section containing carefully graded exercises and controlled activities, which test both global and specific understanding.

Stories from
Greek Tragedies

Retold by Kieran McGovern

1994
Hong Kong
Oxford University Press
Oxford Singapore Tokyo

Oxford University Press

Oxford   New York
Athens   Auckland   Bangkok   Bombay
Calcutta   Cape Town   Dar es Salaam   Delhi
Florence   Hong Kong   Istanbul   Karachi
Kuala Lumpur   Madras   Madrid   Melbourne
Mexico City   Nairobi   Paris   Singapore
Taipei   Tokyo   Toronto

and associated companies in
Berlin   Ibadan

Oxford is a trade mark of Oxford University Press

First published 1994

© Oxford University Press 1994

Retold by Kieran McGovern
Illustrated by Wu Siu Kau
Syllabus designer: David Foulds
Text analysis by Luxfield Consultants Ltd

ISBN 0 19 586305 4

Printed in Hong Kong
Published by Oxford University Press (Hong Kong) Ltd
18/F Warwick House, Taikoo Place, 979 King's Road,
Quarry Bay, Hong Kong

CONTENTS

1

Oedipus the King:
Part One

Apollo speaks

When King Laius and Queen Jocasta of Thebes had their first son, they took the boy to Delphi. Delphi was the place where you could ask the gods for a prophecy for the future. 5

'Will our son be good to us?' asked Laius. 'Will he one day be King of Thebes?'

'This boy will kill his father,' came the terrible answer from the god Apollo.

Laius and Jocasta looked at their tiny baby in horror. 10 Would he one day murder his father?

'There is only one way to stop the prophecy from coming true,' said Laius. 'We must kill him now while he is still a baby.'

'I cannot kill my own child,' whispered Jocasta. 15

But Laius was too frightened to let his son live. He gave the baby to one of his servants. 'Tie his feet together,' he ordered, 'and take him into the mountains far from the city. Leave him in a lonely place where he'll never be found.' 20

'It is winter, my king! The poor child will die.'

'Do what I say or you will pay with your life!'

The Sphinx

Many years later a strange and terrible monster called the Sphinx came to Thebes. The Sphinx was a lion with 25 wings and the face of a woman.

'What is it that walks on four feet, three feet and two feet?' she asked. 'I will die when someone can tell me. But the punishment for the wrong answer is death!'

Many people tried to guess the answer, and were killed. King Laius decided to go to Delphi to ask the gods what he should do. Dressed as an ordinary old man, he left the city with some of his servants. But a few days after he left, a messenger brought bad news back to Thebes. King Laius had been killed by thieves on the way to Delphi. Meanwhile the Sphinx was killing more and more people.

Creon, the brother of Jocasta, spoke on the steps of the palace. 'Anyone who can save us from the Sphinx can marry Queen Jocasta and become our new king,' he said.

That day a stranger arrived at the gateway to Thebes. The Sphinx stood before him.

'Answer my question,' she said. 'What has four legs, three legs and two legs?'

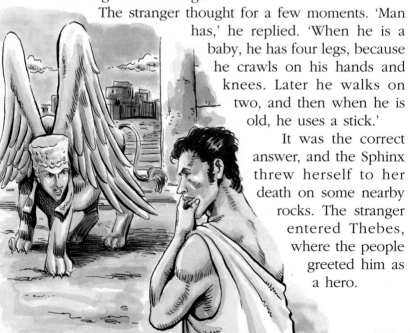

The stranger thought for a few moments. 'Man has,' he replied. 'When he is a baby, he has four legs, because he crawls on his hands and knees. Later he walks on two, and then when he is old, he uses a stick.'

It was the correct answer, and the Sphinx threw herself to her death on some nearby rocks. The stranger entered Thebes, where the people greeted him as a hero.

'Who are you, stranger?' asked Creon. 'Where do you come from?'

'I am Oedipus of Corinth, son of King Polybus and Queen Merope.'

'Oedipus, you have saved our city,' said Creon. 'Will you be our king?'

Plague comes to Thebes

Oedipus married Jocasta. For many years he was a very successful and much-loved king. He was also the father to two girls, Antigone and Ismene, and two boys, Eteocles and Polynices.

Then a terrible plague came to Thebes. Every day more people were becoming ill. All over the city were funerals for both old and young.

No medicine worked against the plague and nobody knew how to stop it from spreading. Many people believed that the plague was a curse.

'The gods are angry,' they said. 'They are punishing us for something we've done.'

A crowd gathered outside the palace. They had come to see Oedipus. They hoped that their king would be able to save Thebes for a second time.

Oedipus came and stood on the palace steps. He looked at the sad and frightened faces before him.

'It breaks my heart to see my people suffering so much,' he said. 'I want to help you. What can I do?'

Creon goes to Delphi

An old man answered. 'Oedipus, our king. We come to you because Thebes is dying. Many years ago you saved us from the Sphinx. Now we beg you to do something about the plague.'

'I promise you I am doing everything I can,' said Oedipus. 'I have already sent Creon, my wife's brother, to Delphi, to ask the gods what we need to do to save our city ... Look, here he comes now. Creon, what message do you bring from the gods?'

'Good news,' said Creon. 'There is a way to save the city.'

'What do we have to do?' asked Oedipus.

Creon pointed to the crowd standing in front of Oedipus. 'Shall we go into the palace? Perhaps I should talk to you alone,' he said.

'No, tell us all!' said Oedipus. 'I have nothing to hide from the people of Thebes.'

'Apollo says that a murder has brought this plague to Thebes.'

Oedipus looked surprised. 'Who was murdered?' he asked.

'Before you came and saved us, our king was called Laius,' said Creon.

'King Laius? Yes, I've heard people talking about him,' said Oedipus, 'though I never met him myself.'

'Well, he was murdered,' said Creon, 'and Apollo says that we must have revenge for his murder. We must find the killer.'

The killer is still in Thebes

'But how can we find him?' asked Oedipus. 'This murder happened many years ago.'

'Apollo says that the killer is still here in Thebes.'

There was a cry of fear from the crowd. But Oedipus waved them to be quiet.

'Where was Laius murdered?' he asked.

'He went to Delphi,' said Creon, 'but he never came home again.'

'And no one saw what happened?'

'No. There were some people with Creon, but they were all killed except one. A servant escaped, but he was so frightened that he could tell us almost nothing.'

'Was there anything he said that might help us?'

Creon thought for a moment. 'He said that a group of thieves attacked them and killed King Laius.' 10

Oedipus shook his head. 'No, this was the work of one man! And what thief would be mad enough to kill a king?'

'That's what we thought,' said Creon, 'but with Laius dead, we had no leader to help us with our problems.' 15

Oedipus looked at Creon angrily. 'Problems? Don't you understand that your king was murdered! Why didn't you hunt down the murderer the very day you heard the news?'

'We were so worried about the Sphinx,' said Creon. 20 'We didn't know what to do.'

'Well, I know what to do,' said Oedipus. 'We must find the killer. Apollo is right, we must have revenge for the king's death.'

Who murdered Laius? 25

Oedipus stood on the steps of the palace and spoke to the crowd.

'Does anyone know who murdered Laius?' he asked.
'If you do know, you must speak now. Even if you are
the murderer yourself, you have nothing to fear. I will
send you away from the city, and we will forget about
the whole horrible business.'

Oedipus stopped and waited for an answer. Nobody
spoke.

'I don't know who you are, but I will find you,'
continued Oedipus. 'And when I do, your punishment
will be worse than death. We will send you from our
city to wander without friends, family or country. You
will be the loneliest man in the world. This is my curse.'

Again there was silence.

'Well, we shall soon know who the murderer is,' said
Oedipus. 'I have sent for the old man, Tiresias. He is
blind, but he can see the truth other men cannot see.
Here he comes now.'

A boy led Tiresias towards the palace.

'Tiresias, you understand what this plague is doing
to our city better than any of us,' said Oedipus. 'You
alone can save us. So tell us the truth! Who murdered
Laius?'

Tiresias shook his head. 'I wish I did not see what I
see. The truth is too painful for any man.'

OEDIPUS THE KING:
PART TWO

The terrible secret

Oedipus looked at the blind old man in surprise. 'What is this you are saying?'

'Send me home,' said Tiresias. 'I cannot answer your question.' 5

'But Tiresias, you must tell us,' said Oedipus. 'The city is dying! We beg you on our knees.'

Tiresias turned away. 'I will not tell such a terrible secret. Especially not to you.'

Now Oedipus got angry. 'You know and you won't 10 tell?' he shouted.

'I don't want anyone to suffer,' said Tiresias. 'So why ask me all these questions?'

Oedipus jumped to his feet. 'I know why you will not tell us!' he cried. 'You are the murderer! Oh, I see 15 it all now!'

'I am blind,' said Tiresias, 'but you are the one who cannot see. You have forced me to tell the truth. The man that we should drive from the city is you. You are the one who has made the gods angry! You are the 20 curse!'

There was a cry of horror from the crowd. Oedipus looked up at the sky and shook his head angrily.

'You stupid old fool!' he shouted. 'What new nonsense is this?' 25

'I say that you are the murderer you are looking for,' said Tiresias.

'A second time you say this terrible thing!' said Oedipus. 'But I am sure that this is not just your work.

Did Creon tell you to tell this lie? Perhaps he wants to destroy me so that he can become king.'

'You are destroying yourself,' said Tiresias. 'Boy, take me home.'

5   'Yes, take the old fool home,' said Oedipus. 'We do not want to see his stupid face any more.'

Oedipus accuses Creon

Creon returned to the palace and stood in front of Oedipus. The king jumped off his throne.

10   'What are you doing here?' he shouted. 'How dare you come here to my palace when I know you are trying to kill me?' Oedipus pointed to the throne. 'You want to sit here in my place, don't you? You want to be king!'

15   'Why would I want to be king?' cried Creon. 'You are married to my sister and I have helped you rule Thebes. We've always worked happily together.'

'You cannot fool me!' said Oedipus. 'I thought you were a friend, but you have been working against me! Well, you will pay with your life!'

'How can you say these mad words?' asked Creon. 'Do you not believe the message I gave you from the gods?

Then go to Delphi and ask yourself. I'd rather die a thousand deaths than betray a friend.'

'Why did you tell me to send for that blind fool who calls himself a prophet?'

'Because he has always been right in the past,' said 5
Creon. 'And he has been here in Thebes since before Laius was king.'

'Then why did he not accuse me of this murder when I first came to Thebes?' demanded Oedipus.

'He has betrayed me!'   10

Jocasta, the wife of Oedipus and Queen of Thebes, heard all the shouting.

'What are you two arguing about?' she asked angrily. 'Aren't you ashamed to be shouting like children when the city is dying?'   15

'Sister, your husband is saying terrible things about me!' said Creon. 'He thinks I have betrayed him.'

'He has betrayed me!' shouted Oedipus.

'I swear in front of the gods that's not true!' cried Creon. 'I would deserve to die if it were.'   20

Jocasta turned to her husband. 'You must believe him, Oedipus! For me!'

'All right, I will let you go,' said Oedipus to Creon. 'But stay away from the palace.'

'I'll leave,' said Creon, 'but everyone knows that you 25
have made a terrible mistake.'

Where the three roads meet

When Jocasta was alone with Oedipus, she asked, 'Why are you so angry?'

'Your brother has told the world that I murdered 30
Laius!' said Oedipus.

'But why does he say such a terrible thing?' asked Jocasta. 'Has he heard a story somewhere?'

'He sent the blind prophet, Tiresias, to accuse me. Creon is too clever to do it himself.'

Jocasta smiled and put her hand on her husband's shoulder. 'A prophet? But who listens to those old fools. No one can say what is going to happen in the future! A prophet once told Laius that his son would kill him.'

'What a terrible prophecy!' said Oedipus. 'What did Laius do?'

Jocasta turned away. There were tears in her eyes. 'He ordered one of his men to leave our three-day-old son on a cold, lonely mountain,' she said. 'But the poor boy died for nothing! Laius was killed by strangers at the place where the three roads meet.'

'Where did you say?' asked Oedipus, looking at his wife strangely.

'At the place where the three roads meet,' said Jocasta. 'That's where he was attacked by thieves.'

Only the shepherd knows

Suddenly Oedipus's face turned white. 'Exactly when was this?' he asked quickly. 'How long ago?'

'Just before you came to Thebes ... What's the matter?' said Jocasta.

Oedipus closed his eyes for a moment. He looked terrified. 'Oh no! The thing I fear is so terrible — I just didn't know!'

'What are you saying?'

'I fear that the blind prophet was not lying,' whispered Oedipus. 'I must find out the truth. Is the servant who saw what happened still in the palace?'

Jocasta shook her head. 'No. When he returned and saw that you were the new king, he was very upset.

He begged me to send
him away from the city.
He is now a shepherd.'

'Can you bring him back?'

'But why do you want to see him?' asked Jocasta.   *5*
'This all happened so long ago.'

A terrible prophecy

Oedipus got up and walked around the room.

'Jocasta, you know that I grew up in Corinth,' said
Oedipus. 'As the son of King Polybus and Queen   *10*
Merope, I lived as a prince. But then one day during a
dinner at the palace, a man who had drunk too much
told me that Polybus was not my real father.'

'What nonsense!' said Jocasta.

'That's what my parents said when I told them. But   *15*
I was still worried, so I secretly went to Delphi to ask
the gods who my parents were. They would not answer
my question, but they made a terrible prophecy.'

'What did they say?' said Jocasta nervously.

'That I would kill my father and marry my mother.'   *20*

'Impossible!' cried Jocasta.

'I hope you are right,' said Oedipus. 'And I've done everything I could to see that such a terrible thing could never happen. When I left Delphi, I didn't return to Corinth. I wandered the world until I arrived at the place where three roads meet. The same place where your king was murdered.'

'That was just chance!' said Jocasta.

'But I did kill someone there,' continued Oedipus. 'An old man in a coach tried to push me off the road. Then he attacked me with a stick. In defending myself, I killed him and his servants. What if this old man was my father?'

'Oh my poor husband!' Jocasta said. 'Don't worry so much! I am sure you didn't kill Laius!'

Oedipus lifted his head. 'There is one thing in the servant's story that gives me hope. He talked about "thieves" — but I was alone! This servant is now a shepherd? Well we must find this shepherd. Only he will know if I am the killer.'

3

OEDIPUS THE KING:
PART THREE

Good news becomes bad news

Oedipus waited alone in his room while his soldiers
looked for the old shepherd. He could not sleep or eat
or think of anything but the terrible prophecy. Could
he really have killed his father?   5

Then Jocasta rushed into the room. With her was a
messenger from Corinth.

'Oedipus, I have good news!' she cried. 'This
messenger tells us that poor old Polybus has died in
his bed. The people of Corinth want you to be their   10
new king. So the prophecy cannot be true!'

'But what about my mother?' asked Oedipus. 'The
prophecy says that I'll marry my mother. And she is
still alive.'

'Don't worry about that nonsense!' said Jocasta.   15
'Forget about the prophecy! Carry on with your life.'

The messenger looked puzzled. 'Who is this woman
you are still afraid of?'

'Queen Merope, messenger!' said Oedipus. 'A
prophecy said that I would kill my father and marry my   20
mother. That's why I left Corinth all those years ago.'

The messenger laughed. 'But Oedipus, you have
nothing to fear. Merope and Polybus are not your real
parents.'

The smile disappeared from Oedipus's face. 'What   25
are you saying?'

'You were a gift to King Polybus,' said the messenger.
'I know because I handed you over myself. You had

been left to die on a mountain near this city. I cut the ropes that tied your feet together.'

Oedipus and Jocasta stared at each other in horror. 'But who did this to me?' asked Oedipus in a strange voice. 'Was it my mother? Or my father?'

'I don't know,' said the messenger. 'The one who gave you to me would know more.'

'Stop asking questions'

'So you took me from someone else? You were not the one who found me?'

The messenger shook his head. 'No, another shepherd passed you on to me.'

'Who was this shepherd?' cried Oedipus. 'Where was he from?'

'He said he was a servant of … now who was it?' The messenger thought for a moment. 'Oh, yes, I remember… King Laius.'

Suddenly Jocasta's face went a terrible colour. Oedipus turned to her.

'Jocasta, is this the same shepherd we have sent for?' he asked.

For a moment Jocasta could not speak. Then she said, 'Does it matter? Why ask? It's just another story told by old shepherds! Don't think about it!'

Oedipus shook his head. 'But I must find out who my real parents are.'

Jocasta took hold of her husband's arm and held it tightly. 'Please, stop!' she cried. 'Stop asking questions! I have suffered enough!'

'No!' said Oedipus. 'I must know it all. When this shepherd comes to the palace, we will know the truth.'

Jocasta screamed and ran out of the room.

The boy on the mountain

Soldiers brought the shepherd into the palace. The old man looked very nervous and unhappy.

'Do you remember me, shepherd?' asked the messenger. 'You gave me a little boy on the mountain.'

'But that was years ago,' said the shepherd. 'Why talk about it now?'

The messenger pointed to Oedipus. 'Because this man here is the very baby you found.' 10

Suddenly the shepherd became very angry. 'Be quiet!' he shouted. 'Keep your mouth shut!'

'Don't talk to him like that!' said Oedipus. 'And tell us what you know about the boy on the mountain.' 15

The shepherd shook his head. 'I cannot tell you anything.'

'Then you will pay with your life!' said Oedipus angrily. 'Answer the messenger's question! Did you give him that child?' 20

'Yes, I did,' said the shepherd, with tears in his eyes. 'And I wish I had died that day!'

'Your wife will know!'

'Where did you get the child from?' demanded Oedipus.
'Was it from your house?'

The shepherd shook his head. 'No, I was given it by ...
5 someone. But please don't ask me any more questions!'

Oedipus moved towards the old shepherd. 'Where
did you get the child from?' he demanded. 'If you do
not tell me, I will have you killed.'

'It was from the house of Laius,' said the shepherd,
10 falling to the floor. 'They said it was his son! But your
wife will know!'

There a short, terrible silence. 'My wife?' whispered
Oedipus finally. 'My wife gave you the baby? But why?'

'To kill it!' said the shepherd.

15 'Kill her own child? But how could she?'

'She was terrified of the prophecy,' said the shepherd.
'The god Apollo said the child would kill his father.'

'But why did you give the child to this messenger?'

'I felt sorry for the baby,' said the shepherd. 'I hoped
20 this man would take him to some country far away.
And then I was with Laius when you killed him. I told
everyone that we were attacked by thieves. But I can
no longer hide the truth!'

Oedipus fell to his knees. 'The prophecy has come
25 true!' he cried. 'I have killed my father and married my
mother. Now the world can see that I am the one who
has cursed this city!'

Oedipus blinds himself

A crowd waited outside the palace. What they had
30 heard was so terrible that nobody spoke.

Suddenly a messenger came running out of the
palace. He was crying and his face was pale.

'What has happened, messenger?'

The messenger put his head in his hands.

'Oh I have just seen something terrible!' he cried. 'Our poor queen ran past all the guards into the palace. She was screaming for dead Laius like a mad woman. Nobody could stop her from rushing into her room and locking the door behind her!

'Fearing what she would do, we tried to force the door open. Then Oedipus came running towards us. Screaming like a wild animal, he knocked the door down. Inside the room we found Queen Jocasta. She had hanged herself!'

The messenger stopped for a moment to wipe away his tears. Then he continued his story.

'Oedipus cut Jocasta down with his sword, and lay her gently on the bed. Then he took the long gold pins that held her dress together. "These eyes will no longer see the pain I have suffered," he cried, sticking the pins into his eyes. "They will no longer see all the pain I have caused!"'

'Send me out of the city!'

A boy led the blind Oedipus onto the palace steps.

'Oedipus, why have you blinded yourself?' cried someone. 'Now your suffering will never end. Is it not better to die than to be blind?'

'My crime was too great for hanging!' said Oedipus. 'How could I look at any man after what I have done? How could I look at my children? How could I look at my father and mother when I join them in the next life?'

Creon came out of the palace.

'Creon, I said terrible things about you,' said Oedipus, 'and I was so wrong! But please do one more thing for me. Send me out of this city now. I want to go where I will never hear a human voice. Oh I will miss my children so much! The two boys will look after themselves, but my two little girls ...'

'Here they are now,' said Creon. 'They have come to say goodbye.'

Oedipus reached down and took the tiny hands of Antigone and Ismene.

'My two darling girls!' he said. 'Thank you for bringing them, Creon. But please send me out of the city.'

'All right, Oedipus, I'll do what you say,' said Creon. 'Let go of your children!'

Oedipus pulled the two girls more closely to him. 'No, please, don't take them away from me!'

Creon ordered his soldiers to separate Oedipus from his children.

'You are no longer king, Oedipus,' he said. 'Once you were the greatest man in Thebes. Now you will wander the world without friends, family or country. Only death will end your pain.'

ANTIGONE:
PART ONE

After Oedipus left Thebes

For many years Oedipus wandered the world as a blind beggar. His daughters, Antigone and Ismene, helped to lead him.

Back in Thebes, Creon ruled until one of the two 5 sons of Oedipus could be king. As they got older, Eteocles and Polynices argued over who would be king, though neither wanted to allow Oedipus to return to Thebes. When Oedipus heard this, he cursed his two sons. The curse was that each brother would kill the 10 other.

The argument between the two brothers grew worse and worse. Finally, Creon helped Eteocles to become king. Polynices was very angry and left Thebes to raise an army to fight against his brother. 15

Meanwhile the gods at Delphi announced that the city where Oedipus died would be the greatest in Greece. Oedipus had now arrived in a place called Colonus, just outside the city of Athens.

Eteocles sent Creon to ask his father to return to 20 Thebes.

'We want you to come home,' said Creon to Oedipus. 'It is not right that you wander the world as a blind beggar. You are dressed in rags and only have Antigone and Ismene to help you. We hate to see you suffer so 25 much! Come back and spend your final days in the city where you were born.'

As Oedipus listened to Creon, he became very angry.

'How dare you come after me like this!' he shouted. 'For all these years you have refused to allow me to return to Thebes. You knew the pain I was suffering, yet you treated me like a criminal! And now you want me to return because you think I can help you.'

'Don't be angry with me, Oedipus,' said Creon. 'It is your son, Eteocles, who begs you to return.'

Polynices wants help

'He is no son of mine,' said Oedipus. 'He did not want to help me when I needed him. Only my darling daughters were with me during the bad times. Now I just want to die here in Athens.'

A little later, Polynices arrived at Colonus.

'Oh poor father!' he cried. 'I didn't know you lived like this. I feel ashamed to see you like this, with only my dear sisters to help you. I know I am the worst man alive.'

Oedipus turned away.

'Sister, why won't he speak to me?' Polynices asked Antigone.

'Poor brother, you must tell him why you've come,' said Antigone

'Yes, you are right,' said Polynices. 'Father, I am older than Eteocles, so I should be king. But my brother has paid the people to give him the throne. And I have been forced out of Thebes. This cannot be right! So I have raised an army in Argos to take back the throne. The gods have said that the city of your final days will be the greatest in Greece. I beg you to come join us in our march on Thebes ... '

Oedipus sends Polynices away

'Enough!' cried Oedipus. 'I don't want to hear any more of your terrible plans. You come to me now because you think I can help you. But where were you when I needed you? Go! Die by your brother's hand!'

Polynices watched his father walk away with tears in his eyes. He turned to Antigone and Ismene.

'My dear sisters,' he said sadly. 'You've heard your father's curse. And I know you will soon return to Thebes. If I die in battle, see that I am buried with honour.'

'Don't do it, Polynices!' begged Antigone. 'Stop your army now and send it back to Argos. You will destroy yourself as well as Thebes!'

Polynices shook his head. 'It's too late!' he said.

'But don't you remember your father's prophecy?' said Antigone. 'He said that you and Eteocles would kill each other with your own swords.'

'I know — but what can I do? My brother, Eteocles, has done me a terrible wrong. I must defend my honour!' Polynices reached out and put his arms around Antigone. 'I must go now.'

'Please, Polynices! Think again!'

But Polynices was already moving away.

'Goodbye, my dear sisters. You'll never look on me alive again.'

A few days later, Oedipus died. He was buried in Athens, the city that was to become the greatest in all Greece.

Brother kills brother

Polynices led the army of Argos in an attack on Thebes. Eteocles defended the city. The attackers were defeated, but the brothers killed each other in the battle.

Now Creon, the brother of Jocasta, became King of Thebes. The new king announced that Eteocles was a hero, and buried him with honour. But Creon refused to bury Polynices, because he had attacked his own city.

Antigone called her sister, Ismene, for a secret meeting outside the palace.

'Oh, Ismene, why do we children of Oedipus have to suffer so much? Have you heard the news?'

Ismene shook her head. 'I haven't heard anything since our two brothers were taken from us in one day.

I know that tonight the armies of Argos have left. But what has happened? I know that it is more bad news from your face.'

Antigone moved closer to her sister. 'People are saying that Creon will not allow anyone to bury Polynices,' she whispered. 'Our brother's body has been left outside the city for the birds to eat. We cannot leave him there.'

'What do you mean?' asked Ismene nervously. 'What can we do?'

'Will you help me bury the body?' asked Antigone.

Ismene looked at her sister in horror. 'You want to break the law of the city?'

'Yes!' said Antigone. 'Polynices is our brother. Nobody will think we are wrong to bury him.'

'Antigone, you know how much our family has suffered in this city. Now we are alone here! If we go against Creon, we will suffer the worst death of all.'

Antigone turned away. 'You don't need to give me excuses,' she said. 'I'll bury him myself. And if I die burying him, it will be an honourable death.'

'Antigone, I'm so frightened for you! Don't tell anyone what you have told me.'

'Why not?' said Antigone, moving back into the palace. 'I want the world to know what I am going to do.'

ANTIGONE:
PART TWO

'Let the birds and the dogs eat him!'

A crowd was waiting outside the palace. Creon came out to speak to the people of the city.

5 'I am here to tell you that the bad days are over,' he said. 'We have won the war, and the two sons of Oedipus died in the battle. By the law of the gods, I am now King of Thebes. You will see if I am a good king by what I do.

'Eteocles died fighting to save our city. He has been 10 honoured with a hero's funeral. But Polynices is a traitor who raised an army to attack the city where he was born. Now he lies on the ground outside Thebes, and that is where he will stay. Let the birds and the dogs eat him! Anyone who tries to bury him will be punished 15 by death!'

At that moment a messenger came running through the crowd. He looked frightened.

'Creon, my king, I have bad news for you,' said the messenger. 'Please do not be angry with me.'

20 'What is this news?' asked Creon. 'Come on, tell us all!'

'I don't know how to tell you this, Creon,' said the messenger. 'But someone has tried to bury the body of Polynices.'

25 'What did you say?' shouted Creon.

'Someone came in the night and did it,' said the messenger, who was shaking with fear. 'Perhaps the gods have decided...'

Creon's face went
red. He was very angry.
'Stop this talk of gods!' he shouted.
'This was nothing to do with gods! Someone did
this for money! And you guards helped him!'
'I swear before the gods that I did not!' cried the
messenger.
'Then find this criminal who has broken my law!' said
Creon. 'Or you shall be the one who pays for this crime
with his life!'

10

Antigone comes before Creon

An hour later the messenger returned.
'We have found the person who has been trying to
bury the body,' he said. 'It is a girl! Guards, bring her
in!'

15

The guards brought in Antigone, and there was a cry
of surprise from the crowd. Antigone walked with her
head high in the air.
'So it was you!' cried Creon. 'My own niece! Did you
do this terrible thing?'

20

Antigone looked straight at her uncle.

'I did something honourable,' she said. 'I buried my brother.'

'And did you know that I had made a law against
5 doing this?' asked Creon.

'Of course,' said Antigone. 'The whole city knew.'

'But you still broke this law!' said Creon angrily.

'The laws of the gods are more important than your laws,' said Antigone.

10 'You are like your father,' said Creon. 'You never listen to anybody. And now you break our law. I am sure that your sister helped you with this.'

Creon gets angry

'Ismene is inside the palace,' said one of the guards.
15 'She is very upset at the news.'

'What more do you want, Creon?' asked Antigone calmly. 'I know you are going to have me killed. '

'How dare you talk to me like this!' shouted Creon. 'I'll see that you die a painful death! And your sister
20 too! Aren't you ashamed to be the only person in Thebes to go against my law?'

'No, I am not ashamed to honour my brother,' said Antigone.

'But Eteocles was also your brother, and he fought
25 against Polynices. He would not want to see the traitor honoured.'

'We don't know that,' said Antigone, 'because Eteocles is also dead. He has been buried with honour. The same should happen to Polynices.'

30 'I will not honour a traitor in the same way as a hero!' said Creon.

'Nobody can say for certain who is good and who is bad,' said Antigone.

'But a traitor will never become a friend!' shouted Creon. 'Not even when he is dead!'

'We should learn to love, not to hate!' said Antigone.

'Then you can learn to love your new brothers and sisters — the dead!' cried Creon. 'I will not allow a woman to stand here and talk to me like this.'

Ismene comes before Creon

Soldiers brought Ismene out from the palace. Her face was wet with tears.

'Here comes the second criminal,' said Creon. 'Tell the city the truth. Did you help Antigone to bury Polynices?'

'Yes, we did it together,' said Ismene, through her tears.

Antigone looked at her sister in surprise.

'But I will be killed, Ismene!
Why should you die too?
You did not help me.'

'But I want to be with you in the danger that is now before you,' said Ismene. 'You are my sister and I love you.'

'No!' said Antigone. 'I buried our brother. I did it alone and I will die alone!'

'Please, Antigone!' cried Ismene. 'Let me die beside you! My life means nothing without you.'

Creon turned to the crowd. 'These two sisters are both mad! Antigone has always been her father's daughter, and now we see that Ismene is just the same.'

'But Creon, my king,' said Ismene, 'how can you think of killing the girl your son wants to marry?'

Creon had only one child, a boy called Haemon. Haemon and Antigone were in love and planned to get married.

'Haemon cannot marry a woman who is dead,' said Creon. 'He will have to find someone else. There are plenty of other girls.'

Ismene cried for Haemon. She knew that the young man loved Antigone very much. 'Creon, this is a terrible thing you're doing to your son.'

'Tie them up!' said Creon to his soldiers. 'And take them away! These women have broken my law and they will die for their crime.'

Haemon talks to his father

Haemon came to see his father.

'My son, have you come to be angry with me?' said Creon. 'I know how much you wanted to marry Antigone.'

Haemon shook his head. 'No, father,' he said. 'I am your son. You are more important to me than any wife.'

'I am happy to hear that, Haemon,' said Creon. 'You have always been a good son. And you will understand that I must have Antigone killed. She has gone against my law. If I do not punish her, others will do the same.'

'I understand, Father,' said Haemon.

'Then forget about Antigone! Find another bride who will make you happy.'

'Father, I am young and you know far more than me,' said Haemon, 'But I am worried about what I am hearing on the streets of Thebes. People are whispering what they do not dare say to their king.'

'What are they saying?'

'That Antigone does not deserve to die,' said Haemon. 'They say that she was right to bury her brother.'

'Oh do they?' said Creon, getting angry. 'And I suppose these people know better than their king?'

'Father, why not think again about this?' said Haemon. 'A good king listens to his people and is ready to change when he sees he is wrong.'

Creon shook his head. 'No. I am the king! I decide what is going to happen in the city. The city belongs to the king.'

Now Haemon was angry. 'You should be the king of a desert island,' he said. 'Then you would only have to listen to yourself.'

Creon jumped to his feet. 'My own son stands here insulting me! You're on her side, aren't you? You've really come to try and save that woman!'

'I see that my father is making a terrible mistake,' said Haemon.

'No! You are making the mistake!' said Creon. 'You will never marry Antigone while she is alive.'

Haemon looked at his father sadly. 'Then her death will lead to my death.'

6

ANTIGONE:
PART THREE

Nothing can save Antigone

'So you say you will kill yourself?' shouted the king. 'Well, we can soon see if you'll do what you say! Guards, bring out Antigone! We'll kill her now!'

5 'No, I will not watch her die!' cried Haemon. 'And you'll never see me again! You are my father, but your mad behaviour is breaking my heart.'

Haemon ran out of the palace.

'Let him go!' said Creon. 'He will not save the two 10 sisters from death.'

There was a cry of horror from the servants standing near the king. 'You are not going to kill Ismene, too?'

'No, you are right,' said Creon. 'Ismene has done nothing wrong. But Antigone will get the punishment 15 she deserves.'

The guards brought Antigone back to Creon. The crowd outside watched in silence. Not one person in Thebes thought that Creon was doing the right thing.

'Take her outside the city,' said Creon, 'and dig the 20 tomb which will be her final home. Leave some food inside, then cover the tomb with rocks so she cannot escape.'

The crowd whispered to each other in horror. This was a terrible punishment.

25 'She can choose whether to die or to live a life buried in the darkness,' continued Creon. 'The decision is hers, not mine.'

Antigone turned to the crowd. 'Look at me, people of Thebes. I am starting my final journey. That sun disappearing from the sky is the last I will ever see.'

'Poor Antigone!' cried someone. 'And today was to be your wedding day.'   5

'Don't cry for me!' said Antigone. 'I will never marry the man I love. I will never have his children. And this tomb will be my final prison where I shall meet the rest of my cursed family. But I know I was right to bury my brother. And I would do the same again.'   10

The guards took Antigone away. The king turned his back on his niece and walked back into the palace. It was almost dark now as the daughter of Oedipus was taken out through Thebes. The people of the city watched in silence. Many had tears in their eyes.   15

Tiresias talks to Creon

Later that night a boy led Tiresias, the blind prophet, into the palace.

'What is it, Tiresias?' asked Creon. 'Why have you come to visit us?'   20

'I have something important to tell you,' said the blind old man.

Creon suddenly felt very nervous. He remembered how Tiresias had tried to tell Oedipus about his terrible past.   25

'I will listen,' said Creon. 'You have always been right before.'

'A prophet looks for signs from the gods,' said Tiresias, 'and what I have seen tells me that something very bad is happening. Birds are behaving very   30
strangely. Their stomachs are full with flesh they have eaten. And they are killing each other across the city.'

Creon did not like what he was hearing. But he tried to pretend that he was not worried. 'So a few birds are dying! There are too many birds in Thebes anyway.'

5 'This dead flesh is from the body of the son of Oedipus. And it is bringing a new plague to Thebes. The gods are angry, Creon. All men should be buried.'

'I am the king here, blind man!' said Creon angrily. 'I decide what is right.'

'You have made a mistake,' said Tiresias. 'And that is only human. But you must do something to correct the wrong you have done.'

'Listen, you old fool!' said Creon, who 15 was both frightened and angry. 'Why have you really come here? Are you looking for money?'

'How can you say this to me, Creon?' said Tiresias, shaking his head. 'After all I have done for this city.'

The king waved his finger at the blind prophet. 'You have helped us in the past,' he said, 'but these days you're more interested in looking for gold.'

'You insult the gods,' said Tiresias, 'and you will pay a terrible price. They will take a life for a life. A son for a son.' The boy led Tiresias out of the palace.   5

Creon agrees to release Antigone

Creon sat for a few moments staring in front of him. Then he went out to speak to the crowd.

'You heard the old prophet,' he said. 'He says that I   10
am wrong.'

'Tiresias has never lied to Thebes,' cried somebody.

'I know this is true,' said Creon. 'But how can I admit that I have made a mistake? I would look like a fool in front of you.'   15

'But you must listen to the prophet, Creon.'

Creon nodded. 'Tell me ... what must I do?'

'Release Antigone from her tomb of rocks!' cried the crowd. 'And bury her brother.'

There was a long silence while Creon thought about   20
his decision. 'It's very hard for me!' he said finally. 'But I will do what you say!'

'Then do it now!' advised the crowd. 'You must hurry! We have very little time!'

The king moved towards the door. 'Come on,   25
everybody. Bring your axes! We will break the tomb open. And I will release Antigone myself.'

Creon goes to the tomb

They went first to bury Polynices. Most of the body had been eaten, so they burned what remained before   30
burying it.

'I hope the Gods will forgive me now,' said Creon.

Then he led the crowd out towards the tomb where Antigone was buried alive. As they got nearer, they heard a terrible scream.

'My god!' cried Creon. 'That sounds like my son, Haemon! It is coming from inside the tomb. Quick, men, move these rocks so that we can go in.'

Soldiers lifted the rocks from the top of the tomb. The screaming grew louder as Creon rushed into the darkness. 'Light me a torch!' he shouted. 'So that I can see what terrible thing has happened here.'

A soldier passed a burning torch to Creon. Now the king could see where the screaming was coming from. To his horror he saw his son in the darkest corner of the tomb. Haemon was still alive, but he had his arms around the body of a dead woman.

Antigone had hanged herself. Haemon had tried to save her, but he had arrived too late.

'Oh my dear child!' said Creon. 'The poor woman is dead. I know she died because of me, but there is nothing you can do. Come away from there!'

Haemon looked at his father with madness in his eyes. Creon moved towards his son, but Haemon took out his sword and tried to kill his father. Then he turned his sword on himself.

'No! Please! No!' cried Creon.   5

But the sword had already gone through Haemon. Creon watched his son put his arms around the bride he had never had. Moments later he was dead.

More terrible news

The body of Haemon was carried out of the tomb.   10
Creon walked beside his dead son. His face was covered in tears and his eyes were red.

'I killed him,' he said. 'I killed my own son by not listening to him. Oh my poor boy! You had your whole life in front of you.'   15

A messenger ran out from the palace. His face was white and he was shaking.

'More terrible news, my king!' he cried.

'What now? What can be worse than losing my only son?'   20

The messenger hesitated. Tears ran down his face.

'The queen is dead,' he whispered. 'The mother of poor Haemon has taken her own life.'

Creon fell to his knees. 'My wife is dead? No! Why me? How can one man suffer so much pain?'   25

'They are bringing her body out from the palace now,' said the messenger.

'What happened? Why did she do it?'

'She killed herself with a sword,' said the messenger. 'And as she was dying, she accused you of killing her   30
only son.'

The body of Queen Eurydice was placed next to that of Haemon.

'It is true!' cried Creon. 'I murdered them both! You, my young son … You too, my wife! All because I would not listen to what the city was telling me.'

Tiresias returns

5　A boy led Tiresias out from the crowd. The blind prophet stood on the palace steps and spoke to the people of Thebes.

'Here is a story about a man who had everything,' he said. 'Creon saved the city from the army of Argos.
10　He became King of Thebes. Now he has lost his son and his wife. He has paid the highest price for breaking the law of the gods.'

Creon turned to Tiresias.

'Tiresias, you tried to tell me, but I would not listen.
15　I insulted you and sent you away. But now I have suffered enough!' Creon pointed to the crowd. 'Tell them to kill me! I don't want to live with this memory.'

'No,' said Tiresias. 'You are still king, Creon, and the curse of the house of Oedipus continues.'

20　'What are you saying, prophet? That there is more bad news to come?'

'A new army is coming from Argos,' said Tiresias. 'And this time you will not have Eteocles by your side. You will face the new attack completely alone. That is
25　all I want to say.'

The boy led Tiresias away from the palace and away from the city. Later the armies of Argos attacked Thebes. This time they won the battle and took Thebes.

MEDEA:
PART ONE

Medea is crying in her room

When the teacher arrived back with the two boys, it was getting dark. He could hear the sound of crying from Medea's bedroom. On the front step, the family nurse was sitting with her head in her hands. 5

'What's wrong, nurse?' he asked. 'Where is Medea? Is she still alone in her room? Has she not stopped crying?'

The nurse looked up. 'How can she stop crying after what has happened to her? Do you know the story of 10 how Jason and Medea came to Corinth?'

The teacher looked down at the two boys, and then back at the nurse. 'Medea fell in love with Jason,' he said in a low voice. 'She was so in love with him that she helped kill his enemy, King Pelias. She left her 15 family and her country to come with Jason to Corinth. She gave him two sons. But —'

'This afternoon Jason married the daughter of the King of Corinth!' said the nurse. 'He has left Medea and his two sons to live in the palace!' 20

'Poor Medea! And she has not heard the worst news!'

The secret

'What has happened?' asked the nurse.

'I've heard that the King of Corinth is going to send the boys away from here,' said the teacher. 'He wants 25 their mother to go, too!'

'But what about Jason?' asked the nurse. 'I know that
he is angry with Medea, but they are his sons too. Surely
Jason would not allow them to send his sons out of the
city!'

5   The teacher laughed at this idea. 'Jason doesn't care
about Medea and her family now. He thinks only of his
new wife. He is no friend of this family.'

The nurse looked at the children. 'Run into the house,
boys,' she said sadly. 'Everything will be all right.'

10   As the children moved towards the house, the nurse
turned to the teacher.

'Keep the boys away from their mother until these
bad times end,' she said. 'Medea is suffering terribly.
Who knows what she'll do next!'

15   From inside the house Medea's voice was getting
louder. 'What shall I do?' she cried. 'I want to die!'

'Listen to your poor mother, children!' said the nurse.
'Go into the house, but stay away from her. When she
is this angry, she can do terrible things.'

20   **'Death to all in his house!'**

While the teacher put the boys to bed, the nurse went
and stood outside Medea's room.

'Are you all right?' she asked.

'They all hate me!' cried Medea.
'My children are cursed! Death to
them! Death to their father!
Death to all in his house!'

'Medea, this is so sad!' said the nurse. 'It is Jason who has been wicked, not his children! Why hate them?'

But Medea was not listening. 'I left my father and my city for Jason!' she cried. 'I gave up everything for him! And now he has left me!'

The nurse went to get the teacher. 'Oh I am frightened, teacher!' she said. 'Listen to the terrible things Medea is saying.'

'I want to die!' came the terrible cry from Medea's room. 'I want Jason and his princess to die for what they have done to me!'

'You must try and calm her,' said the teacher. 'Everyone in the city understands why she is so sad and angry. But this terrible talk can only end in terrible things.'

'I'll try and talk to her,' said the nurse, 'but these days she does not listen to anyone.'

Creon visits Medea

When Medea finally came out of her room, she was calm. She was not crying and did not look angry.

'You have all seen what has happened,' she told the nurse. 'Jason was my whole life, but now we can all see that he is the worst of men. He has left me and I have nothing. I want to die.'

'You have suffered terribly,' said the nurse.

'Men have the best of this world,' said Medea. 'A wife can only have one husband. She must hope that he is a good man. But if a man gets tired of his wife, he can go and get another one!'

'This is true,' said the nurse. 'And it cannot be right. But look who is at the door! It is Creon, King of Corinth.'

Medea walked out to meet Creon. The old king stared down at his shoes. 'Medea, you cannot stay in Corinth,' he said. 'Take your sons and leave this city. I will not return to my palace until you have gone.'

5 'This is a cruel end to my life,' said Medea. 'Where can I go? Everywhere my enemies wait for me. Creon, why are you doing this to me? What have I done to deserve this punishment?'

'I am afraid of what you will do to my daughter,' said 10 Creon. 'You're a clever woman who knows how to do terrible things. Jason has left you and you are angry. And everyone knows that you have been talking of revenge!'

Medea laughed and shook her head. 'Don't listen to the stories people tell, Creon,' she said. 'There are many 15 in this city who are jealous of me because they think I am too clever.'

Medea must leave the city

'You are a dangerous woman,' said Creon, 'And I don't want to give you the chance to take revenge on my 20 family.'

'But what can I do to you, Creon?' asked Medea softly. 'I am just a weak woman! It's true that I hate my husband, but I do not have any argument with you or your daughter. I wish you both good luck. Please let 25 me live in Corinth, Creon!'

'Your words are gentle,' said Creon, 'but I know you have wicked plans in your heart. In fact, I trust you much less now than before. An enemy who is mad with anger is less dangerous than one who is quiet and 30 clever. So leave the city now! I don't want to hear any more talk —'

Medea fell to her knees. 'How can you do this to me?' she cried.

'Because I love my family more
than anything in the world!'
said the king. 'Now go, or
I will tell my soldiers
to take you away!'

'No, please, Creon!' begged Medea.
'I have just one thing I want to ask of you!'

'Medea, I don't want to hear any more clever words,'
said Creon. 'You must go!'

'I will go, Creon!' cried Medea. 'I promise in front of   10
Zeus, our god. But let me stay just one more day. I
need to make plans for my two sons. Creon, you are a
father too, so feel pity for them! I don't care about
myself, but I will cry for those poor boys. How they
will suffer!'   15

The king was not a cruel man. And he did feel pity
for the two boys. Medea was a dangerous enemy, but
the children did not deserve to suffer.

'My soft heart has often betrayed me,' he said, 'and
I know it's foolish of me now. Medea, you will have   20
the time you ask for. Even you cannot do what I fear
in just one day.'

MEDEA:
PART TWO

Medea plans revenge

'Poor Medea!' said the nurse when the king had gone. 'Where can you go now?'

Medea walked to the window and looked out onto
5 the city. Then she turned and said, 'Things will not stay as they are. I have plans for my husband and his pretty young wife.'

'But you only have one day,' said the nurse.

Medea laughed cruelly. 'I have all the time I need,' she
10 said. 'Why do you think I begged Creon to let me stay?'

The nurse saw a strange look in Medea's eyes and felt frightened. 'What are you going to do?' she asked.

Medea turned back to the window. She looked out and saw Creon's palace in the distance. Pointing
15 towards the palace, she said, 'Today I will kill my three enemies: the king, his daughter and my husband. I haven't decided how I shall kill them yet. Shall I set fire to the house and burn them in their beds? Or shall I put a knife through their hearts while they are asleep?
20 No, they will not allow me into the palace. It will have to be poison.'

'Medea, forget this idea of revenge. It can only end in more suffering!' said the nurse. 'But look who comes towards the house. It is Jason!'

25 ### Jason arrives from the palace

Jason came into the house, shaking his head angrily at Medea.

'Medea, you have caused more trouble for yourself!' he said. 'You could have stayed in Corinth and lived in this house. All you had to do was to accept that I have a new wife. Instead you talked like a fool, and now the king has sent you away.'

'Is that right, Jason?' shouted Medea. 'You leave your wife and children! You destroy my life. And yet I am the one who has done wrong?'

'You are lucky, Medea,' said Jason. 'After what you've been saying about the king and the princess, you are lucky they have not killed you. I have tried to calm them down, but it has been very difficult. Why do you keep saying these wicked things about the king and his family?'

'Get out of my house,' said Medea angrily.

Jason shook his head sadly. 'I know you hate me,' he said. 'But I want to help you and the children if I can. You will need money to start a new life in a new city.'

'You coward!' screamed Medea. 'You are my worst enemy and you've come to my house. Everybody knows that I saved your life when you came to my island. And what have you done for me?'

Jason and Medea argue

'Medea, why talk about these things now? Why can't you accept that our life together is over?'

Medea was not listening.

'I even gave you two sons!' she shouted. 'But you still went off to find yourself another wife. And where can I go now? Everywhere people hate me because of what I did for you. You have a new wife and live in a palace, while I must take your sons to beg for a home somewhere in the world. Can that be right?'

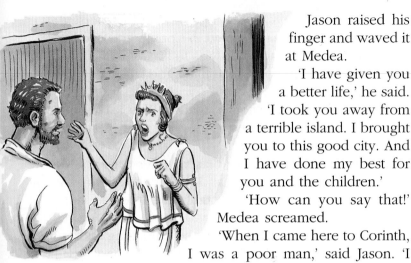

Jason raised his finger and waved it at Medea.

'I have given you a better life,' he said. 'I took you away from a terrible island. I brought you to this good city. And I have done my best for you and the children.'

'How can you say that!' Medea screamed.

'When I came here to Corinth, I was a poor man,' said Jason. 'I was very lucky to get the chance to marry the king's daughter. And do you know why I married her?'

'Because you were tired of me and wanted a pretty new wife!' said Medea.

'No!' said Jason, 'I married her so that we could live well. I did not want us to stay poor. I wanted our two boys to grow up in a comfortable home. And I wanted them to have more brothers. You cannot have any more children, can you?'

This was a cruel thing to say. In Corinth no woman was allowed to have more than two children.

Jason does not understand

'So I married the princess for you and the children,' said Jason. 'One day you'll see that I was right, and understand that you've been very lucky. Don't blame me for what has happened! Blame yourself! It was you who cursed the king and his house.'

Medea moved closer to Jason and whispered, 'Yes, it was. And I cursed your house, too.'

Jason began moving back towards the door. He was famous in all Greece as a brave soldier. But he did not understand why Medea was so angry.

'I don't want to argue any more,' he said. 'I'll gladly give you and the children anything you want. Or I can send letters to friends in other cities. I'm sure they can help you.'

'I don't want anything from you,' said Medea, 'and anyone who is your friend is my enemy.'

'You refuse my help because you are so madly jealous,' said Jason. 'But the gods can see that I've done my best to help you and the children.'

'Go!' screamed Medea.

Medea meets Aegeus

Aegeus, the King of Athens, was going to Delphi to ask the gods for a son. As he passed through Corinth, he met Medea.

'Medea, you look very unhappy!' said Aegeus.

'Aegeus, my husband has betrayed me. He has left me for another woman. And I was always a good wife to him.'

'But that's terrible!' said Aegeus, shaking his head.

'It is the worst thing in the the world,' said Medea sadly. 'Once he loved me, but now I mean nothing to him.'

'You must forget about him then,' advised Aegeus, 'and start a new life here.'

Medea shook her head. 'That's not possible. The father of his new wife is Creon, King of Corinth, and Creon is sending me away from Corinth.'

'And Jason has done nothing to stop this?'

'He has tried to talk to Creon,' lied Medea. 'But the king will not listen.'

'I wish I could help, Medea, but…'

'You can help,' said Medea quickly. 'You are King of Athens, the greatest city in Greece. Let me come and live there, and the gods will thank you with a son. I

5   know a special medicine which I promise will help you and your wife have a child.'

Aegeus hesitated. There was something

10   about what Medea was saying that made him feel a little nervous. But he did want a son very much, and Athens was a city which always tried to help people who were in trouble.

'I will help you if you can get to Athens,' he said

15   finally. 'But I won't help you leave Corinth. The people of Athens have no argument with the people of Corinth.'

'That is all I ask,' said Medea.

MEDEA:
PART THREE

Medea sends for Jason

'Oh nurse, things are going my way at last!' said Medea, laughing and dancing around the room. 'Aegeus is going to help me with my plan!'

'I don't understand,' said the nurse.   5

'You'll soon see!' said Medea. 'But first, send a slave to tell Jason I want to see him.'

An hour later, Jason arrived at Medea's house. He came in and saw that Medea was sitting with her head in her hands. She looked very sad and there were tears   10
still wet on her face.

'I have come as you asked,' he said, 'and I'm ready to listen. What do you want?'

'Oh, Jason, I'm sorry!' she said. 'I did not mean the things I said to you. I was just very upset. I know that   15
you are trying to do your best for me and the children. And of course I don't want an argument with the king.'

The two children came into the room. Medea called them to her and then pointed to Jason. 'Go to your   20
father and put your arms around him.'

'I am happy to see that you now think this way, Medea,' said Jason, 'and of course I understand how you felt before. Women often don't like it when their husbands marry a second wife. But now you have made   25
a good decision... What's the matter?'

Medea was staring at her children and crying as if she was in pain.

'Why are you crying?'

Gifts for the princess

Medea could not tell him the truth. She was crying because she knew that something terrible was going to happen to her children.

5　　'I am worried about the children,' she said. 'I'm their mother,' she explained, drying her tears, 'and mothers always worry. But there is one more thing that I must ask you.'

Jason let go of the two boys and they moved towards
10　their mother. She put her arms around them.

'I know that I have to leave Corinth,' said Medea, 'but I would like the children to grow up with you. Will you ask Creon to let them stay?'

'I'll try,' said Jason, 'but I don't know whether the
15　king will agree.'

'Your wife could ask her father to let them stay,' said Medea.

'That's a good idea,' said Jason. 'I'm sure he will listen to his only daughter.'

'And I can help,' said Medea. 'I'll send gifts to your wife. The most beautiful gifts in the world. The children can take them to her. Nurse, go and get the dress and the golden crown.'

A few moments later, the nurse returned with the gifts. Medea passed them to the two boys. 'Now my darlings, take these gifts to the palace. Give them to your father's new wife with your own hands.'

The princess accepts the gifts

Later that morning the teacher returned with the
children. He was smiling and looked very happy.

'Good news!' he shouted, as he came through the
door. 'The boys can stay here in Corinth. The princess   5
took your gifts from them and was very happy. They
have no enemies in the palace.'

Medea stared at him without saying anything.

'How cruel!' she whispered. 'How cruel life is.'

The teacher shook his head. 'I don't understand,' he   10
said. 'I thought that this was good news. Why are you
crying?'

'When you see what I have done,' said Medea, 'you
will also cry. Now leave me alone with the boys.'

Medea put her arms around her children and kissed   15
them.

'Oh my poor boys! I must go away and never see
you again. It breaks my heart! Oh I can't look at you
any more. Go to your room, my darlings.'

Suddenly a messenger from the palace rushed into   20
the house.

'Oh Medea!' cried the messenger. 'You must run
away, escape! What a terrible thing you have done!'

'Why should I escape? What has happened?'

The terrible gifts   25

'It is a terrible story!' said the messenger.

Medea laughed. 'Then I will enjoy it more! Tell me
everything, messenger!'

'When your two little boys arrived at the palace with
their father, everyone was happy. We knew that you   30
had been treated badly, and we were glad that you and
Jason were friends again.'

Medea laughed more loudly. 'You fools!'

'I followed Jason and the children to the princess's room. At first she did not want to see your boys. But then Jason said, "You must love what I love. Take the gifts that my children bring, and allow these boys to stay here in Corinth."'

'And what did she say?'

'When she saw the beautiful gifts, she agreed. She loved them so much that she tried the dress on straight away. And putting the golden crown on her head, she began walking up and down in front of the mirror. Then we saw a horrible, horrible thing!'

'Oh, good news!' cried Medea. 'Tell me all.'

'The princess changed colour and began falling across the room. Her eyes turned completely white and a strange liquid came from her mouth. The dress and the crown were poisoned!'

'Of course,' said Medea, 'she had to die! What happened then?'

'For a few moments we just couldn't believe what we were seeing,' said the messenger. 'Then a servant ran to get King Creon. Everyone was running and screaming. And the poor princess was in terrible pain as the poison ate her skin.'

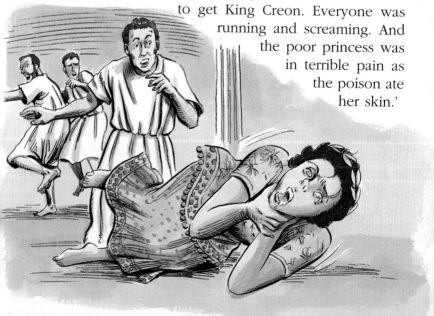

Medea clapped her hands. 'I would love to have seen it!' she cried.

'Then the king rushed to his daughter and tried to lift her. But the poison joined his skin to that of the princess. Father and daughter did a horrible dance of death across the floor. And there was nothing anyone could do!'

'My plan worked!'

The messenger looked at her in horror.

'But Medea, how could you do such a thing?'

'It was a just revenge,' said Medea calmly, 'and the gods are with me. Now I must leave Corinth, but first I have one last thing to do. I must kill my two sons!'

The nurse, who had come into the room, cried out in horror, 'No!'

'If I do not kill them, someone else will. I love them more than anything in the world. I gave them life, and now I must take it away. Life is cruel.'

Jason arrives too late

Jason ran towards Medea's house. The teacher and the nurse were sitting on the steps with their heads in their hands. The front door was locked.

'Is Medea still in the house? Or has she escaped? There is nowhere in the world she can hide from my revenge. She has killed the king and the princess! She must be punished!'

'Jason —'

'Where are my children? I have come to save them before Creon's family murder them in revenge for this terrible crime of their mother's.'

The nurse spoke through her tears. 'Jason, we have more terrible news. Your sons are dead. Their mother has killed them.'

Jason ran at the door. 'Let me in!' he screamed. 'Let me see my dead sons!'

Suddenly Medea appeared above the roof. She was sitting in a chariot pulled by dragons. The bodies of her
5 two dead children were beside her.

'It is over, Jason!' she said calmly. 'I am taking my sons to be buried in Athens.'

'Why have you done these terrible things, Medea?'
10 cried Jason. 'You will suffer too. They are our children. My loss is your loss.'

'It is true,' said Medea, 'but I was ready to suffer any pain to get justice. You betrayed me and now we have all paid the price.'

15 'The gods will punish you for this terrible crime!'

But the chariot was disappearing into the clouds. Medea was already on her way to the new life Aegeus had promised her in Athens.

ELECTRA:
PART ONE

The sacrifice of Iphigenia

Greece was at war with Troy. King Agamemnon of Argos was about to lead the Greek navy into battle. A thousand ships waited in the port of Aulis.

Agamemnon called his young daughter, Iphigenia, to see him. 5

'Come with me to Aulis and watch our great navy sail off to war,' he said.

But when they reached Aulis, Agamemnon took Iphigenia to a temple. 10

'Oh great gods, I give you this sacrifice to help us win the war!'

Then he took his sword and killed his daughter. When Queen Clytemnestra, the wife of Agamemnon and the mother of Iphigenia, heard the news, she cried for days.

'I will never forgive him!' she whispered to herself. 'One day he will pay for this crime.'

The murder of Agamemnon

After a war lasting ten years, Agamemnon and the Greeks finally won the war. Agamemnon told his army to rob Troy of all its treasure. Then he ordered his
5 soldiers to burn the city.

Agamemnon returned to Argos as a hero. He took back to his palace all the treasure stolen from Troy, and many slaves that he had taken prisoner. He also brought back a woman from Troy called Cassandra.
10 Agamemnon told Clytemnestra that he now wanted two wives.

Clytemnestra pretended to welcome Agamemnon and his new wife. But in her heart she was still very angry about the death of her daughter. Now her
15 husband had insulted her by bringing Cassandra back to the palace. She hated Agamemnon enough to want to kill him.

Agamemnon was also hated by his cousin, Aegisthus. Many years before, Agamemnon's father had
20 argued with the father of Aegisthus over who was to be king. Agamemnon's father had killed the brothers of Aegisthus, and sent his father out of the city.

Together, Aegisthus and Clytemnestra planned their revenge. Clytemnestra continued to pretend that she
25 was happy to see her husband back in the palace. Then, one terrible night, she and Aegisthus murdered both Agamemnon and Cassandra.

Orestes and Electra

Aegisthus married Clytemnestra and became king. But
30 many people in Argos were horrified at the murder of Agamemnon. They especially hated the queen for having betrayed her husband.

The new rulers were nervous. Aegisthus was worried about Orestes and Electra, the son and daughter of the murdered king. They had been young children when Agamemnon went off to Troy, but Aegisthus feared they would one day want revenge for the murder of their father.

The new king tried to have Orestes killed, but an old servant of Agamemnon helped the boy escape. The servant took the boy to King Strophius of Phocis, a city on the other side of the mountains. So the young prince grew up outside of Argos, and apart from his sister.

Electra was allowed to stay at home. As she got older, many important young noblemen wanted to marry her. But Aegisthus was still nervous, because any prince Electra married might want revenge for the murder of her father.

'I do not trust her,' he told Clytemnestra. 'And I fear that she may even try and have a secret son of noble blood. Such a boy could grow up with revenge in his heart. I say we kill her now before she can do anything to us.'

But the queen did not want her second daughter to die.

'I helped kill my husband,' she said, 'because he was a cruel man who did terrible things to me. But I cannot kill my child! Think how people will hate me!'

'Then I have a new plan,' said Aegisthus. 'I'll offer gold to anyone who finds and kills Orestes. And Electra can marry a man who does not have noble blood. Someone who will not be a danger to us.'

Electra and the shepherd

So Aegisthus married Electra to a poor shepherd. The princess was forced to leave the palace and live in the hills away from the city. She was very unhappy, though her new husband was a kind, gentle man.

'I know I am not your true husband,' said the shepherd. 'So we do not have to live as man and wife.
5 You can have your own room in my cottage.'

'You are very kind, shepherd,' said Electra. 'You are my only friend in this cursed world. My father's murderers are living in his palace. And my own mother has driven me out of the city.'

'One day your brother will come back to help you!' said the shepherd. 'But Electra, you do not have to work so hard. You are a princess.'

'Dear shepherd, you have been so kind to me,' said
15 Electra. 'I want to do what I can to help you. You have work to do on the farm, so I shall look after the cottage and make it comfortable for you.'

The shepherd went off into the hills to work with his sheep. Electra went to get some water from a nearby
20 well. As she carried the jug back to the house, she talked to herself.

'What a terrible life I have now!' she cried. 'The shepherd is a good man, but I am alone all day in this cold and lonely place. People in the city call me "poor
25 Electra"! Oh, I wish my brother would come and punish the people who have done this to me.'

A friend from the city

An old friend from the city came out to visit Electra.

'Electra, I have come to invite you to a festival. It's happening in the city the day after tomorrow. All the girls of Argos are going to Hera's temple.'

Electra pointed at her clothes. 'How can I go to a festival dressed in the rags of a poor country girl? I have no fine dresses or gold necklaces. Look at me — I have no comb for my hair, and no soap to wash it!'

'Oh please come!' said the friend. 'Hera is always a great festival. I can give you a lovely dress and a gold necklace to go with it.'

Electra shook her head. 'My days and nights are spent crying!' she said. 'I can't go off dancing. I have to do the right thing for my father's memory.'

'But crying will not do any good. You cannot bring your father back! Don't spend all your time thinking about revenge. Pray to the gods to help you start a new life! Although you wear those old clothes, you are still a young and beautiful princess.'

But Electra began to move away from her friend. 'No, I must continue to suffer,' she said. 'The gods will not listen to me. My brother should be king, but he lives in another man's house. While I live in the cottage of a poor shepherd, the murderers of my father live in his palace. I can have no life until I have justice.'

11

ELECTRA:
PART TWO

Orestes is secretly in Argos

Orestes had grown up in Phocis in the palace of King Strophius. He had been happy living there, but he knew that one day he would have to do something about the
5 murder of his father. When he was eighteen, he went to Delphi to ask the gods to advise him. Apollo told him to return to Argos and kill his father's murderers. In his heart, Orestes doubted whether this was the best thing to do. But he was afraid to go against Apollo.

10 So Orestes secretly returned to Argos with his friend, Pylades. The two young men hid in the countryside outside the city.

'I am worried that someone will recognize me,' he explained to Pylades. 'And I am looking for my sister.
15 I am told that she has married a shepherd and lives near here. I have not seen her since she was very little,' said Orestes. 'But now I need her help to get revenge on my father's murderers. But look, here comes a slave carrying a jug of water. Quick, hide!'

20 Orestes and Pylades tried to hide behind a bush. The 'slave', who was really Electra, saw them and began to run.

'Don't run away!' called Orestes. 'We're not here to hurt you.'

25 But Electra was terrified. 'Oh Zeus, our great god! Don't let them murder me!'

'Don't be afraid!' said Orestes. 'I will kill my enemies. But you are no enemy of mine.'

Orestes reached out and took Electra's hand.

'Keep your hands off me!' she cried. 'Who do you think you are?'

'Someone very special to you,' said Orestes.

Electra tried to push him away. 'How can that be?' she demanded. 'You are a stranger!'   *10*

News of Orestes

Orestes smiled. 'I come with news of your brother,' he said. Suddenly the expression on Electra's face changed completely.

'If you have news of Orestes,' she said, 'then you   *15* certainly are a friend! Is he alive?'

'He is very much alive,' said Orestes.

'And what country does he live in now?'

'He travels from city to city,' said Orestes. 'There is nowhere he calls home.'   *20*

'Do you have a message from him?'

Orestes looked at Electra for a moment. Then he said, 'He wants to know what kind of life you have.'

Electra was still young and beautiful. But she felt old and ugly.   *25*

'Look at my face,' she said. 'It has been destroyed by my tears. And I've cut my hair off.'

'For your lost brother and your dead father?'

Electra sighed. 'They mean more to me than anything in the world!' she said.   *30*

'Electra, why do you live so far from the city?' Orestes asked.

'I came here when I was married,' said Electra.

'But who are you married to?'

5   Electra pointed to the shepherd's cottage. 'This is where I live. I am married to a poor shepherd. He is a good man and knows that he is not really my husband.'

Orestes looked angry. 'And your mother is happy to see you living like this?'

10   Electra sighed. 'She cares about her new husband, not her children. But one day Orestes will come himself and take revenge.'

'And would you help your brother to kill your mother?' asked Orestes.

15   'Of course!' said Electra. 'I would kill her with the same axe that killed my father.'

The shepherd returns

Orestes felt a little ashamed to hear his sister talk like this. Electra believed that her brother was going to
20   come and murder Aegisthus and Clytemnestra. But Orestes still doubted that this was the right thing to do.

'I wish Orestes was here to hear you,' said Orestes.

'I would not recognize him,' said Electra. 'We were both very young when he went away. Only the servant
25   who saved his life would know him now.'

'But tell me, Electra,' said Orestes, 'what has been happening since Orestes left?'

'Many terrible things,' said Electra. 'I was treated like a slave, while my mother sat on her throne wearing silk
30   dresses and gold jewels. And people say that Aegisthus sometimes jumps up and down on my father's grave.'

The shepherd returned and found them all standing outside the cottage.

'Dear husband,' said Electra, 'these two men are friends of Orestes.'

'Friends, you must all come into my cottage,' said the shepherd. 'I have always been poor. But I'll give you what food and drink I have.'

Electra whispered to the shepherd, 'Go and find the old servant who saved my brother. I'm sure he would love to meet a friend of Orestes.'

Later that morning the old servant arrived at the cottage. Electra went out to greet him.

'Dear Electra, my princess,' said the old man, 'I am always happy to see the daughter of my old master, Agamemnon.'

But Electra saw tears in the old man's eyes. 'Why are you crying?' she asked.

Who visited the grave?

'On my way here,' said the old man, 'I passed your poor father's grave. I knelt down and cried for my king. Then I noticed that there were new footprints leading up to the grave. I looked closer and saw that a chicken had been sacrificed. There was even a piece of hair offered to the gods! Someone has been there!'

'But who could it have been?' asked Electra. 'Nobody in Argos would dare visit my father's grave.'

KING AGAMEMNON OF ARGOS

'Perhaps your brother went there secretly,' said the old man. 'To show his love for your poor father. Go there yourself and see if the colour of the hair is the same as yours. Brothers and sisters often have the same
5 colour hair.'

'Nonsense!' said Electra. 'My brother would never come here secretly. He is certainly not at all afraid of Aegisthus! And it's not just brothers and sisters who can have the same colour hair.'

10 'Then see if the footprints are like your own,' said the old man.

Electra laughed. 'Footprints? How could there be footprints with all those rocks there? And a boy's footprints are always bigger than a girl's.'

15 ## The shepherd recognizes Orestes

Orestes and Pylades came out of the house.

'Here are the two friends of Orestes,' said Electra. She turned to Orestes and Pylades. 'Friends, this is the man who saved my brother.'

20 The old man looked closely at Orestes.

'Why is he looking at me like that?' asked Orestes nervously.

Suddenly the old man put his arms around Orestes. 'Oh thank the gods!' he cried. 'You have come back
25 to Argos!' He turned to Electra. 'This is the man you are waiting for!' he cried. 'This is Orestes!'

Electra did not speak for a moment. Her face turned white.

'My brother? she said finally. 'No! I don't believe it.'
30 'But look at the scar on his head!' said the old man. 'Don't you remember that day when you were playing together in the palace? Your brother fell and cut his head.'

Electra continued to stare at her brother. She had been praying for his return for so long! It was so difficult to believe that he was now standing before her.

'Yes, I see it!' She moved forward to take her brother in her arms. 'Dear Orestes! I thought you would never come!'

'I have come for revenge!'

For a few moments Orestes and Electra stayed in each other's arms. After so many years apart, they were more like strangers than brother and sister. Neither knew what to say.

'I have waited so long for this happy day,' said Orestes. 'I almost gave up hope of seeing you again.'

'Brother, I prayed for your return every day.'

Orestes moved out of his sister's arms. 'We have work to do, sister! I have come to hunt down the criminals who forced us apart.'

'There is nothing I want more!' said Electra. 'We will make our father's murderers pay a high price.'

Turning to the old man, Orestes said, 'Old man, you were a good servant to my father. I have come for revenge on those who murdered him. Tell me what I should do next. Do I have any friends in Argos?'

The old man shook his head sadly. 'No. You have been away too long,' he said. 'Nobody in Argos will help you return to your father's house.'

'Then what must I do?'

'Kill Aegisthus and your mother,' said the old man.

Orestes nodded. 'But how? Is the palace very well guarded?'

'Yes,' said the old man. 'Aegisthus is so frightened of you he cannot sleep at night.'

ELECTRA:
PART THREE

How to kill Aegisthus

'Is there any way to get past his guards?' asked Orestes.

The old man thought for a moment. 'Yes, I think there could be one way. When I was coming here, I saw
5 Aegisthus in a field with some of his servants. It looked as if he was going to sacrifice a bull.'

'Good news,' said Orestes. 'But how can I get close enough to kill him?'

'When he is sacrificing the animal, you must stand
10 nearby,' advised the old man. 'He will invite you to join the party.'

Orestes nodded. 'And where is my mother?'

'She's still in Argos. She's afraid of the people of the city! They hate her because of what she has done,' said
15 the old man. 'But she'll join her husband for the sacrifice.'

'So do I kill them both at the same time?' asked Orestes.

'No, I want to kill my mother!' cried Electra. She
20 turned to the old man. 'Go to Clytemnestra and tell her that I have just given birth to a son. Ask her to come and see the new baby.'

'Do you think she will come?' asked the old man.

'Yes, she'll come,' said Electra. 'And when she does,
25 I'll kill her. But first you must take my brother to Aegisthus.'

'I'm ready to kill him,' said Orestes. 'Come, Pylades, our hunt for my father's murderer is nearly over. The old man will show us where we can find him!'

'Kill him, dear brother,' said Electra, as the three men moved away. 'And if you die in this honourable work, I shall take a sword to my own heart.'

The sacrifice

Aegisthus was standing with a group of his servants in a field. He was offering a bull as a sacrifice to the gods. When he saw two strangers standing nearby, he called out, 'Where are you from, strangers?'

'We are Thessalians going to Delphi,' lied Orestes.

The king smiled. 'Come and join our party,' he said. 'We are killing this bull to offer to the great god, Zeus. You Thessalians are said to be great swordsmen. You can help us cut up the animal.'

Orestes and Pylades walked over to join the party. Aegisthus offered Orestes a sword.

'Friend, I have just cut the throat of this bull,' he said. 'Will you cut the rest of the animal? Then we can all eat together.'

Orestes cut the bull open. When the blood poured onto the floor, the king suddenly looked very worried.

Orestes kills Aegisthus

'What's the matter?' asked Orestes.

'Friend, I see signs in the blood of that animal!' said Aegisthus nervously. 'I fear that Agamemnon's son will try and kill me.'

Orestes laughed. 'But he lives far away from here!' he said. 'How can Orestes kill you? Bring me a bigger sword and I'll cut this animal up properly.'

A servant brought Orestes a bigger sword. Orestes hit the bull again.

The old man bent down to pick up the pieces of meat. Orestes lifted his sword again. This time he cut into Aegisthus' neck.

There was a horrible scream. The king's guards took out their swords and moved towards Orestes and Pylades.

'Guards, I am not an enemy of Argos,' cried Orestes. 'This man murdered my father, so I have punished him. I am Orestes. You men were once my father's servants. Are you going to kill me now?'

There was a moment's silence. Slowly the guards began putting their swords away. Then they began to cheer and put flowers around the neck of the man who had killed Aegisthus.

'Are we going to kill our mother?'

'Welcome, my brave brother!' cried Electra. 'Welcome, Orestes!'

Orestes stood before her. He held in his hand the head of Aegisthus. Beside him was Pylades. Some servants carried the body of Aegisthus.

'I have killed him, dear sister,' said Orestes. 'Do what you want with his body.'

'I have waited so long for this day,' said Electra. 'But take the body away! My mother must not see it before we cut her throat.'

'Clytemnestra is coming this way!' said Pylades.

They all looked down towards the city. Four horses were pulling a golden coach. Inside was Clytemnestra, with her servants.

Electra laughed cruelly. 'How well she lives, with her golden coach and her fine dresses.'

Orestes turned to his sister. 'Are we really going to kill our mother?'

'Of course!' said Electra angrily. 'Why not?'

'She gave me life,' said Orestes. 'How can I kill her?'

'How?' Electra laughed. 'In the same way she killed our father.'

Orestes shook his head. 'Apollo was wrong to tell me to kill my mother,' he said. 'But what can I do? Perhaps the gods will punish me if I do not do what they say.'

'Don't be a coward!' said Electra. 'Go and wait in the cottage.'

'I will do it,' said Orestes. 'Though I feel in my heart that I should not.'

Mother and daughter

Clytemnestra got out of her coach and stood before Electra. She looked old and weak.

'I know you hate me, daughter,' she said. 'But your father caused all your problems. You had a sister you never knew. He murdered her! Then he brought home another woman from Troy.'

'I don't want to hear your stories,' said Electra.

'Electra, you have always loved your father,' said Clytemnestra sadly. 'I forgive you. I killed your father because I was so angry at what he had done to me. It is something I now regret.'

'It's too late for regret!' said Electra. 'And why do you not bring Orestes back to Argos?'

Clytemnestra turned away. 'I am terrified of him,' she said. 'People say he wants revenge for his father's death. But let's not talk of such things. Tell me, child, why did you send for me?'

'I want you to see my baby,' said Electra. 'Come into the house and I'll show you him.'

The queen hesitated. 'I really should go and join my husband. He is making a sacrifice near here.'

'Come and see my baby,' repeated Electra. She opened the door of the shepherd's cottage. 'It will only take a minute.'

As Clytemnestra passed through the door, Electra picked up a sword she had hidden behind a bush. It was the sword that had killed Aegisthus, and it was covered in blood.

'What have I done?'

Servants carried the body of Clytemnestra out of the cottage. Electra and Orestes followed behind. They looked horrified.

'Oh, gods! What have I done?' cried Orestes. 'I have killed my mother!'

'Brother, blame me!' said Electra. 'When the moment came, I could not use the sword. But I forced you to do this terrible crime!'   5

Orestes fell to his knees beside his mother's body. 'Where can I go?' he cried. 'Who can look at a man who has killed his mother?'

'And who will marry me now?' cried Electra, kneeling next to her brother. 'Oh mother, we love you, though   10 we hated you!'

Suddenly there was a flash of light in the sky. The god Castor appeared before them.

'Orestes, you must go to Athens and explain to the gods about this terrible crime,' ordered Castor. 'Apollo   15 told you to kill your mother, but you should have listened to your own heart. You will never be able to return here to Argos.'

Electra bowed her head in front of the god. 'Castor, I deserve the greater punishment! It was I who said she   20 must die!'

'Electra, you will marry Pylades and live in Phocis. Take the shepherd with you and make him a rich man. You will never see your brother or your country again.'

Orestes turned to his sister with tears in his eyes.   25 Electra and Orestes had grown up strangers. Even when they killed together, they did not know each other. Now they really loved and needed each other for the first time. But they would never be together again.

'I lose you,' he said, 'and you lose me. That is the   30 worst punishment that the gods could give us. But it is what we deserve.'

QUESTIONS AND ACTIVITIES

CHAPTER 1

Put these words in the right gaps to say what happens in this part of the story: **ordered, gods, prophecy, king, nobody, monster, murder, thieves, stranger, answered.**

When King Laius and Queen Jocasta went to Delphi, they heard a terrible (1) _____. Apollo told them that their son would (2) _____ his father. Laius (3) _____ a servant to leave the baby on the side of a mountain. Years later a (4) _____ called the Sphinx came to Thebes. The Sphinx asked a question which (5) _____ could answer. Laius went off to ask the (6) _____ at Delphi, but was killed by (7) _____. Finally a (8) _____ came to Thebes and (9) _____ the Sphinx's question. The stranger married Jocasta and became (10) _____.

CHAPTER 2

Put the letters of these words in the right order to say what happens next.

Tiresias, the blind prophet, came to the (1) **elapca**. He did not want to answer Oedipus's (2) **nsotqeuis**. But Oedipus insisted that Tiresias tell the (3) **uhtrt**. Tiresias said that Oedipus was the (4) **drmuerer**. Oedipus then (5) **dseaucc** Creon of betraying him. But when Oedipus learned how Laius was (6) **dkille**, he became very (7) **tenfirghed**.

CHAPTER 3

Put the beginnings of these sentences with the right endings to say what happens next.

1 The messenger told Oedipus
2 A servant of Laius gave
3 Jocasta screamed

a) and ran out of the room.
b) the baby to King Polybus.
c) the son of Laius and Jocasta.

4 The messenger gave

5 Oedipus was really

6 Oedipus left Thebes

d) to wander the world.

e) he was not the son of Merope and Polybus.

f) the baby to the messenger.

CHAPTER 4

Put the words at the end of these sentences in the right order.

1 Oedipus wandered the world   [beggar] [a] [as] [blind].

2 Both Eteocles and Polynices   [king] [to] [wanted] [be].

3 Creon would not bury   [body] [Polynices] [the] [of].

4 Ismene thought it was too   [dangerous] [break] [Creon's] [to] [law].

5 Antigone had tried   [bury] [the] [body] [to] [Polynices] [of].

CHAPTER 5

All these statements are false, except one. What should the false ones say?

1 Haemon did not like Antigone.

2 Haemon thought his father was wrong.

3 Ismene told Creon that she did not help to bury the body.

4 Creon thought that a king should listen to the people.

5 Creon said that he did not have to punish Antigone.

CHAPTER 6

Put these sentences in the right order to say what happens in this part of the story. The first one has been done for you.

1 Tiresias told Creon that the gods were angry with him.

2 Queen Eurydice killed herself.

3 Creon buried the body of Polynices.

4 Creon admitted that he had been wrong.

5 Creon went to the tomb where Antigone was buried.

6 Haemon killed himself with his sword.

7 Haemon found Antigone dead in the tomb.

CHAPTER 7

Some of these sentences are true, but others are false. Which are the false ones?

1 Medea was very happy that Jason had married the princess.
2 The nurse was worried about Medea.
3 King Creon asked Medea to come and live in his palace.
4 Creon ordered Medea to leave Corinth.
5 Creon was afraid of what Medea would do to his daughter.
6 Medea told Creon she would burn his palace down.

CHAPTER 8

*Who said these things? Choose from **the nurse**, **Jason** or **Medea**. You will need to use one name more than once.*

1 'I want to help you and the children,' said ————.
2 'And where can I go now?' asked ————.
3 'I have given you a better life,' said ————.
4 'Forget the idea of revenge!' said ——————.

CHAPTER 9

Choose the right words to say what this part of the story is about.

Medea sent her (1) **sons/nurse** to give the presents to (2) **Creon/the princess**. The presents were (3) **very nice/poisoned**. When the messenger came back from the palace, Medea was very (4) **sad/pleased**. Both the king and the princess were (5) **dead/ill**.

CHAPTER 10

Put these paragraphs in the right order.

1 Agamemnon returned to Argos as a hero. He took back to his palace all the treasure stolen from Troy, and many slaves that he had taken prisoner.
2 Clytemnestra pretended to welcome Agamemnon and his new wife. But in her heart she was still very angry about

the death of her daughter. She hated Agamemnon enough to want to kill him.

3   After a war lasting ten years, Agamemnon and the Greeks finally won. Agamemnon told his army to rob Troy of all its treasure. Then he ordered his soldiers to burn the city.

4   Greece was at war with Troy. King Agamemnon of Argos was about to lead the Greek navy into battle. A thousand ships waited in the port of Aulis.

CHAPTER 11

Put the beginnings of these sentences with the right endings.

1 Electra wanted the old man	a) that someone had visited the grave.
2 The old man had seen	b) by the scar on his face.
3 Electra recognized Orestes	c) for revenge.
4 Orestes said he was in Argos	d) to meet two friends of Orestes.

CHAPTER 12

Choose the right words to say what this chapter is about.

1   The old man knew a way to get past Aegisthus's **wife/guards**.
2   Aegisthus was **chasing/sacrificing** a bull in a field.
3   Orestes killed Aegisthus with **a sword/poison**.
4   Clytemnestra arrived in a golden **cloud/coach**.
5   Electra told Clytemnestra her baby was in the **cottage/field**.

Oxford
Progressive
English Readers